"What a lovely dog!" Joe thought. He'd always wanted a dog like that.

The dog yapped again. Joe laughed.

"I'm going to buy you for my birthday," he said.

Inside the shop, there were rabbits and hamsters and puppies and kittens and mice.

There were budgies in cages and goldfish in a tank.

A snake lay curled up in a glass cabinet and a spider crawled in a jar.

Joe reached down to the dog in the window. It licked Joe's fingers.

Joe knew this was the dog for him.

"I'm going to take you home," he said.

"Take me home!" squawked a parrot on a perch.

"No way," Joe said.

He didn't want a parrot. He wanted a pet he could take for walks and teach tricks.

Joe went to the counter.

"Can I help you?" said Mr Parker.

"I want to buy that dog," Joe replied. He couldn't wait to get it home. What would he call it?

Mr Parker shook his head.

"Sorry," he said. "Not that one."

"Why not?" said Joe.

"It's not the right dog for you, lad. I have some much nicer pets."

Mr Parker pointed
to some puppies in
a basket. "How about
one of those?"

"I don't want a puppy,"
said Joe. He looked
at the window.
The black and white
dog stared back with
its big brown eyes.

"How about a parrot?"
said Mr Parker.

"Me! Me!" the parrot
squawked.

"Or a nice
hairy spider?"

The spider
crawled in its jar.

"I don't *want* a parrot," said Joe, shaking his head. "And I don't *want* a spider. I want that lovely dog."

"Silly boy!" squawked the parrot. "Silly boy!"

"I'm not silly!" said Joe, trying to ignore the parrot.

"Please don't talk to my parrot like that," said Mr Parker.
"He'll get upset."

"But *I'm* upset!" said Joe. He had the money. Why couldn't he have
the dog?

The parrot flew over to Mr Parker's shoulder and squawked:
"Silly boy!"

Joe wished he could leave the shop and get away from the parrot, but
he didn't want to go without the lovely dog. He imagined cuddling up to
him on the sofa. He'd be his best friend. What a lovely birthday present!

Joe didn't know what to do. He glared at the parrot. He glared at Mr Parker.

"Not me!" squawked the parrot as it flapped its wings.

Mr Parker frowned at Joe and stroked the parrot's head. "Now look what you've done. You've upset Polly!" he said.

"But I just want the dog. I don't care about your silly parrot," said Joe.

Mr Parker's frown disappeared. The corner of his mouth curled up in a smile. He'd had quite enough of this boy. "I'll tell you what," he said slowly. "If you apologise to Polly, you can have Monster for free."

"Who's Monster?" asked Joe.

"The dog," said Mr Parker, smiling.

"Why would you call a lovely dog Monster?" asked Joe.

Mr Parker shrugged. "It was just a name I liked."

Joe didn't really mind – he could change the dog's name when he got home. Maybe he'd call him Bouncer. Or Bright-eyes.

"I'm sorry," Joe said quickly.

Mr Parker shook his head. "Say it like you mean it."

Joe sighed. "I am really really really sorry, Polly," he said.

"Silly boy!" Polly replied.

Joe grinned as Mr Parker went to the window to get the dog. He handed him over to Joe.

Joe gazed into the dog's shining eyes. The dog barked and licked Joe's hands. He couldn't wait to get him home!

"Bye," said Mr Parker. "Have fun!" Joe was too busy stroking his new dog to see the twinkle in his eye.

Joe carried Monster out in his arms. The dog licked Joe's hands. It nibbled his fingers with its sharp little teeth.

Joe laughed. "Stop it," he said. The dog barked and struggled in Joe's arms. Joe put the dog on the ground.

"Be nice!" he said.

The dog barked louder. It nibbled at Joe's ankle.

"Ouch!"

Joe started to run but the dog ran after him.

"Please, get off me!" said Joe.

Perhaps Monster was the right name for the dog after all!
"GET OFF ME! OUCH!"

Joe kept on running. The dog kept on running after him.
"CAN I GIVE HIM BACK?" yelled Joe.

Mr Parker just waved from the pet shop door. "Goodbye, Monster," he said.

"Silly boy," squawked Polly. "Silly silly boy."

Things aren't always what they seem

Ideas for reading

Written by Gillian Howell
Primary Literacy Consultant

Learning objectives: *(reading objectives correspond with Gold band; all other objectives correspond with Copper band)* read independently and with increasing fluency longer and less familiar texts; infer characters' feelings in fiction; empathise with characters and debate moral dilemmas portrayed in texts

Curriculum links: Citizenship

Interest words: ignore, frown, apologise

Resources: pens, paper, drawing materials

Word count: 793

Getting started

- Ask the children if they have any pets and dogs in particular. Ask them to describe what they are like and what they do.

- Read the title together and discuss the cover illustration. Ask the children what animals they can see and where they think the boy on the cover is.

- Turn to the back cover and read the blurb together to confirm the children's ideas. Ask them to suggest what might happen to Joe and the dog in the story.

Reading and responding

- Ask the children to read the story quietly and remind them to use their knowledge of phonics and familiar words to work out words they are unsure of.

- At the end of p15, ask the children to describe what has happened so far. Ask them to suggest why they think Mr Parker has changed his mind about giving Joe the dog.

- Ask them to suggest why they think the dog's name is Monster and what might happen next, then read to the end of the book.